Golden Ribbons

Miss Demeanor Series
Book 4

Lauren Marie

EXCERPT FROM GOLDEN RIBBONS

Cassie wanted to give this guy a swift-kick. "God, Mr. Negative, who died and made you the expert? Do you work vice?"

"No, drug task force, and I know these streets. Your girl is probably in Bangkok by now."

"You don't know shit. She was seen here just last Friday. Get your stick out of your ass and tell me what you know about Sally Skinner." Cassie felt ready to pull her Glock out and shoot this guy in the foot.

"Sally Skinner works for Fred and Rick Powell, two of the biggest drug traffickers in the Northwest. A lot of people have died because of them."

When Cassie heard the name Fred she felt on the right track. "One of this kids friends said she was being watched by some guy named Fred. I've heard of the Powell's. I worked drugs down in Arizona..."

"Yeah, if those pansy-asses down in Arizona and Texas kept the doors closed to Juarez and Nogales we wouldn't have this situation up here." He leaned against the dumpster and stared, again. She wanted to slap him across the cheek just to wake him up. "Sally has a cat-house in Slut Alley down in Sodo. She keeps her kids there or at a house up on Beacon Hill."

Dedication

Joanne Jaytanie, Jackie Marilla and Angela Ford - Thank you for the invite. I look forward to more from our Detectives.

Look for Lauren Marie's other titles

I'm Not What You Think

The Canon City Series - Love's Embers - book 1, Love on Ice - book 2

One Touch at Cob's Bar and Grill - the Montana Ranch Series

Love's Touch - Then and Now

Going to Another Place

:

Chapter One

Cassie Holmes drove her beat-up 2010 Jeep Wrangler across the Evergreen Point Floating Bridge. She'd never driven on a toll road and never on a bridge that floated on a lake. Hoping all the checks and balances were in place, she looked out at the water and swallowed. It was a big damn lake and the last thing she needed this week would be a huge ticket for not paying a toll.

She headed away from Seattle to the east side of Lake Washington to the city of Bellevue where she'd been hired to find a fourteen-year-old girl who'd disappeared. It was her first job out as a private investigator and she wasn't sure which direction to go first.

Having just relocated from Prescott, Arizona to Seattle, Washington turned into a huge shock to her system. She'd come to Seattle for a vacation with three friends and the weather pulled the wool over their eyes. During their visit, the days were warm and sunny and the nights cool. Now it rained for ten days straight and she felt a little like the zombie apocalypse might start at any moment. She knew her tan suffered and she'd have to break down and find a tanning salon.

On top of that, she'd come from employment as a drug task force detective run by the State of Arizona, to partner in Miss Demeanors Private Detective Agency. She felt fifty-fifty on her decision to make this change, but also knew she wouldn't miss the politics at the Prescott cop house. She'd worked as a patrol officer for her first five years and then passed her detective boards and worked another five years. At thirty-one years of age, after bashing her head against the promotion brick wall, she'd been frustrated and angry. Everything with the opening of the Miss Demeanor Agency went so smooth, it felt like a dream.

She followed her GPS directions and found the apartment building of the woman that came to her group's office last night. The poor woman spent an hour and a half on the Metro bus to get to their office in Pioneer Square. Cassie felt bad about that, but the woman's story could have made blood from her heart run out of her eyes.

Emily Cane married a jerk who beat her up routinely. He'd injured her so bad she'd needed to have back surgery. She'd gotten hooked on painkillers and after being in la-la land for three years, she'd checked herself into detox and gotten clean. When she got home, she learned her jerk husband abused her fourteen-year-old daughter, Cami Reynolds. The daughter started to hang out with older kids and one day disappeared. Emily Cane left the jerk husband, moved to low-income housing and searched for her daughter since.

Cassie hated being a sap and did her best to hide it, but the woman's story killed her. She believed Emily told her the truth and made it her duty to find Cami.

She parked in a guest spot outside the apartments and walked toward the section with the correct number. Emily contacted some of Cami's friends and now

Cassie planned to question them. She knocked on the apartment door.

Her client answered her knock with, "Hi, Miss Holmes. Thank you so much for coming."

Cassie walked into the small apartment and scoped out the situation. To the left was a one-butt kitchen and a tiny dining room with a small two-seat table in the corner, and to the right a living room with a loveseat, TV and two chairs. The carpet looked old and Cassie thought she smelled mold, but couldn't be sure. They didn't have a lot of mold in Prescott.

Emily handed her an envelope. "These are some pictures of Cami. I should have brought them yesterday, but forgot. Her school picture from last year is in there. It's the most recent."

"Thank you, these will help. Did you persuade her friends to come over?"

"Yes, they're waiting out on the deck in back. Come this way." Emily walked to a door Cassie didn't notice at first and opened it onto an outside porch.

She walked past Emily and introduced herself to the kids. There were two boys—Jimmy and Kit— with current haircuts and a lot of tattoos. The one girl—Patrice—wore enough makeup for three models and a lot of piercings. They all wore what Cassie guessed was current clothing. She didn't realize combat boots were still in fashion.

"Please call me Cassie." She smiled at the kids. "How long have you been friends with Cami?" she asked first. It was imperative to make the kids feel relaxed enough to talk.

They spoke for a half hour about how they'd met in elementary school, but didn't start to hang around each other until last year. Things changed though a couple of months ago when she started to go out with the older kids. All three of Cami's friends looked at Emily and Cassie felt they were holding back and probably didn't want to upset Cami's mother. They either knew something important or felt they shouldn't say anything at all.

Cassie stood up and put her notepad and pen into her jacket pocket. "I'm hungry. Why don't we walk up to the McDonalds at the corner? My treat."

"Are you through?" Emily asked.

"No, we're going to go for a walk. Is it okay for me to leave my Jeep parked in a guest spot?"

"Yeah, it's fine. Do you want me to come along?"

"No, I'll check back with you before I leave."

She and the kids walked silently down the street to McDonalds. She bought them sodas and French fries and they sat in a booth. Cassie pulled the notebook back out.

"Okay, so what aren't you telling me?"

The boy Jimmy looked at the others and played with a straw. "Cam started hanging around some really bad   kids."

"Yeah, she'd do just about anything to get out of her mom's house. Ben wasn't treating her right," Patrice said with big soulful brown eyes lined like an Egyptian.

"Some nights they'd go into Seattle and party. She started to miss classes," Jimmy continued. "She changed a lot."

"When was the last time you saw her?" Cassie asked.

"It's been about two months, maybe longer for me."

Patrice looked at the two boys. Jimmy nodded, but the other boy who spoke very little seemed uncomfortable.

"Please, Kit, I just want to make sure Cami is safe."

"I saw her last Friday under the freeway at the waterfront."

"What part?"

"Just up from the ferry terminal. It's called *Slut Alley*. She said she'd been taken in by some woman named Sally, but it turned into a nightmare. The woman isn't the real boss, but she didn't tell me who was running things. She wants to leave, but someone won't let her."

"You mean she couldn't come back with you?"

"She said she was being watched by some guy named Fred. I guess she tried to run away, but he found her and beat her up pretty good."

Cassie pulled her new business cards out of her bag and handed them to the kids. "If you hear from Cami, call me or have her call me. I want to help."

"You're going to get her away from those people, right?" Kit asked.

"I do want to try."

"I don't think she'll come back if her stepdad is still around."

"No, he won't be around. Mrs. Cane left him. She told me how he'd treated Cami. He isn't there anymore and Mrs. Cane is cleaned up. Cami won't have anything to worry about."

The kids went quiet. Cassie didn't think they had much more to offer. "I have one more question. As far as you know, is Cami drugging?"

They looked at each other and Jimmy said, "Cami watched what drugs did to her mom. She hates how Mrs. Cane acted. She took an oath with all of us that we'd never use."

Cassie nodded. "Good. If you guys think of anything else, give me a call at any time." She got a little more information and then parted ways with the kids. She walked back to Emily Cane's apartment, gave her a brief update and then left.

It took her two hours to get back to Pioneer Square. There was an accident on the bridge and she inched along in the traffic. It gave her a little time to think about what she'd learned about the missing girl and to plot her course of action. Cassie's heart hurt for all the poor kid went through. No one deserved that kind of treatment. Her hope became saving the girl. It would make everything she'd done in the last six months, worth it.

As she got closer to the agency, Cassie decided to head down to the waterfront and have a look around. She'd never been down there and it was time to get her feet wet.

Chapter Two

He sat on a barrel under the viaduct and knew he looked intimidating and scruffy. Several others sat around the beat up property. There was a drunken debate raging about starting a fire to warm up, but that would bring in the patrolmen. He felt cold with the rain, the coat he'd snagged from Goodwill barely fit or kept him warm and dry. He held a fifth of what was supposed to be cheap, bargain-basement whiskey. He'd poured most of it out and filled the bottle with black tea. It left just enough alcohol in the mix that the other homeless folks wouldn't see him as anything but another drunk.

His dark brown hair hung down below his shoulders and he couldn't wait for this case to end just so he could cut his hair and shave. The damn beard itched. Jack Donovan worked undercover for a Seattle

Drug Task Force for the last five years. He'd been a cop for nine years and this was the longest case he'd ever worked. For the most part, he liked the job, but he'd been out here for six months and really just wanted to go to his house up in North Seattle and mow the lawn. Catching the bad guys made him feel like a superhero sometimes, but he'd never admit that to anyone.

Jack saw a good-looking woman stroll out on the sidewalk. She stopped people and showed them what must be a picture. *She's probably some loser parent looking for a runaway,* he thought.

But she wasn't just another woman. She looked tall, maybe five-foot-eight or nine with medium blonde hair to her shoulders. Her face looked tan so he figured she might be an out-of-towner looking for some lost family member. What really caught his eyes though, were her legs. The pants she wore were only slightly loose around her ass and thighs, and he could tell she worked out. At times like these, he didn't like undercover work. He looked and smelled like a Sasquatch and no way could he walk up to a good-looking woman and ask her out.

She stopped a woman who held a garbage bag and showed her the picture. The garbage bag lady shook her head and handed the picture back.

The woman stepped off the sidewalk and walked toward where he and the other characters sat around. When he saw the way she walked, it was obvious she carried a gun under her left arm. She was a cop.

She glanced around at the group of people. "Excuse me. I'm a private investigator and I'm looking for a missing kid. Have any of you maybe seen this girl?" She handed the picture around to those closest to her and got negative responses. She crossed her arms and leaned on one of her legs. "Do you have a minute to answer some questions?"

Jack thought she might be new to this type of work. Trying to look and act all nice wouldn't work under the viaduct.

"Are you some sort of Beagle?" Willie asked and gave her a toothless grin. Jack thought the old guy must be in his nineties and had no idea what Willie meant by his question. He felt ready to defend her if the man called her a dog.

She gave Willie a confused look. "I'm not sure what you mean."

"You know, like a gumshoe or private dick?" he groused and continued to show his rotten gums.

"Oh right, you mean a sleuthhound. Yeah, that's what I do." She handed Willie the picture.

He looked at it and shook his head. "Ain't never seen her, but she's a pretty little thing, isn't she?" He handed her the picture back.

The woman moved around the group and finally came to Jack. She held up the picture. "Have you seen her?"

He didn't look at the photograph and stared at the woman. "Nope."

"You didn't look at it."

"Sure I did. Saw it with my third eye."

"Don't talk to him, lady. He's an asshole and won't share his booze," one of the other men said.

He felt impressed by this woman. She didn't back down and break the stare. Yep, she'd been a cop, he could tell it as well as he could breathe.

She smiled and still held the picture up. "Are you some kind of big-ape-asshole like your friend says?"

"He ain't no friend of mine," the other guy said, got up and left.

She arched her eyebrow and turned her back to him. "Have any of you heard of a handler named Sally? She pulls kids off the street for prostitution."

"Lady, you don't want to mess with Sally Skinner. She's in tight with the Powell boys and they pretty much run this neighborhood."

"Do you have any idea where I can find her? I heard there's a place called Slut Alley?" the woman continued to press.

Jack stood up and walked past her. He bumped her shoulder and kept walking. When she brought up Sally Skinner's name, he figured it would be best to set her straight. If that lying bitch got her hands on the kid the woman was looking for, there probably wouldn't be much left to find. Sally used the kids for perverted sex addicts, got them strung out on drugs and then shipped them off to Hong Kong or Bangkok.

He hoped she'd follow him, but didn't want to break out of character and look back at her. Walking down an alley, he stood behind a couple of dumpsters. While he waited, he put the cap back on the top of his bottle, stowed it in his pocket and lit a cigarette.

After a minute, he heard footsteps crunch on loose gravel.

"I know you're here. I can smell your smoke and body odor."

He moved from behind the dumpster and flicked his cigarette butt away. "What's your name?"

"Cassandra Holmes. You?"

"Miss Holmes, you might as well give up. You're chasing a lost cause."

****

Cassie wanted to give this guy a swift-kick. "God, Mr. Negative, who died and made you the expert? Do you work vice?"

"No, drug task force, and I know these streets. Your girl is probably in Bangkok by now."

"You don't know shit. She was seen here just last Friday. Get your stick out of your ass and tell me what you know about Sally Skinner." Cassie felt ready to pull her Glock out and shoot him in the foot. She knew he tried to intimidate her with his height. It wouldn't work. She was tall, too and didn't have to look up at him much.

"Sally Skinner works for Fred and Rick Powell, two of the biggest drug traffickers in the Northwest. A lot of people have died because of them. Fred's hobby is prostitution—the younger the better. The guy's sick."

When Cassie heard the name 'Fred', she knew she was on the right track. "One of this kid's friends said she was being watched by some guy named Fred. I've heard of the Powell's. I worked drugs down in Arizona..."

"Yeah, if those pansy-asses down in Arizona and Texas kept the doors closed to Juarez and Nogales, we wouldn't have this situation up here."

"Focus, please. Where can I find Sally Skinner?"

He leaned against the dumpster and stared, again. She wanted to slap him across the cheek just to wake him up.

"Sally has a cathouse in Slut Alley down in Sodo. She keeps her kids there or at a house up on Beacon Hill."

"How does she get away with this shit? Does she have connections with the chiefs on your force?"

"She wishes. She's pretty good at covering her ass."

"What is Sodo and how do I find the cathouse?"

He went silent and continued to watch her.

Maybe this guy is really drunk, she thought.

"Have dinner with me," he finally said.

Cassie felt her eyebrows crease and then laughed. "You wish. How do I find Sally Skinner's place?"

"You don't want to go there. It's guarded pretty tight and can be dangerous. You might break a nail."

It became very apparent to her, this man wasn't going to help. She turned and started to walk away.

"Wait a minute, where are you going?" He moved in front of her and blocked the way.

"I'm going to find someone willing to be helpful."

"Miss Holmes, what part of *dangerous* don't you understand? Your tiny handgun under your left arm pit is a pea shooter compared to what you'd see down there. We'd be pulling your body out of the Sound in the morning."

"Look asshole, not that I need to explain anything to you, but my pea shooter is a Glock Seventeen and I've been known to hit a bull's-eye at two-hundred yards with a Smith and Wesson Rapid-fire. Don't fuck with me, dude."

"Wow, you get sexy when you talk guns."

"Shut up." She walked around him and headed back the way she came. "Asshat," she mumbled as she turned right. She could see Safeco Field and decided to go in that direction. It quickly became clear to her that Sasquatch followed.

Cassie turned around, put her hand on her Glock inside her holster, but didn't pull it out. She stared at him. "I will shoot you if you continue to follow me."

He held up his hands and took a step back. She continued away from him and heard him mumble words at her, but she couldn't understand. She felt certain she didn't want to know what he said.

Chapter Three

Cassie returned to the agency and found the door locked. She took her keys out of her pocket, opened the door and trudged her way in. She didn't hear the chime over the door when it opened. Dropping her bag, keys and jacket on her desk, she hit the On button for her computer and went in search of coffee. There was the sound of someone sighing in the direction of the conference room and Cassie went to see who still hung around.

Looking through the door, she saw her partner, River Nightingale, sitting at the end of the table surrounded by stacks of papers and folders. She went through the door and flopped into one of the plush leather chairs.

"Hey."

"Hey back."

"The chime isn't working on the front door."

"I turned it off. It started to buzz and I'm going to have Cory call to get it fixed tomorrow." River looked over at Cassie and smiled. "How'd the first day on your new case go?"

Cassie snorted. "I met Bigfoot today."

"Wow, so Bigfoot *is* real?"

"Yeah and he's a cop working undercover down by the viaduct. Go figure, right? All those hunters wasting time up in the mountains and it turns out Sasquatch is a city boy." They both laughed. Cassie stretched her legs out and pushed her shoes off. "As first days go, it was better than my first day at the academy. I got a lead, maybe." She looked at her partner. "We'll see what happens tomorrow; I have some research to do and am in desperate need of caffeine."

"The pot's half full in the kitchen, but it's been cooking most of the afternoon. You may want to make a fresh batch."

"Ah, burned coffee, my favorite. What are you doing?"

"Paperwork. I'll introduce you to it once I get my head wrapped around some way to organize it. I know I should let Cory do this, but I felt like one of us should know how to find a folder we might need."

"So, Gage must be working tonight?"

"And there's that, too." River smiled.

"Okay then. Hi-ho, hi-ho, it's off to research I go." Cassie picked her shoes up and stood.

After she got herself a cup of coffee and went to her desk, she signed onto the computer, pulled her notebook out and looked at the notes. During the next several hours, she dug up what she could find on Sally Skinner, the Powell boys and the Seattle street kid scene. By the time she felt she'd done enough, she had seventy-four pages of printed material to look through and needed to rest her eyes from staring at the computer screen.

Pulling her cell phone out, she clicked it on and saw two messages. One was from her mother down in Arizona which turned out to be a *hope all is going well* call. The second message being from her partner, Shay. She hit the play button and listened to the message.

"Hey girlfriend. Tomorrow, Wednesday, five in the morning, Volunteer Park. See you there unless I hear otherwise."

Cassie looked at the clock on her computer and saw it was after eleven o'clock. It seemed like a good time to quit for the night. She'd have a good run in the morning and then start her day on a fresh note.

The next morning Cassie got up at four-thirty, and put on a pair of gray sweat pants and navy blue hoodie. She drove to Volunteer Park and found her partner stretching at the path opening.

"Good morning, Shay. Ready for me to beat you back?" Cassie asked as she put her keys in the hoodie pocket.

"Yeah, right. Those long legs of yours can't keep my pace," Shay joked. "Stretch it out, not that it will help you at all." Shay grinned and put her foot up on a tree and leaned over it.

"Oh, that sounds like a challenge to me. Are we doing five today?"

"Not an inch under."

They ran the five miles side by side. On the uphill parts of the path they slowed their pace a little and compared notes on their cases. She filled Shay in on Sasquatch.

"It's too bad you didn't get his name. We could have looked up his service record," Shay said as they topped the hill.

"Yeah, but he was so arrogant. He wasn't much help, just an annoyance."

"Maybe if he got the beard shaved off, cut his hair and took a shower he wouldn't seem so egotistical?" Shay laughed and raised her eyebrows.

"Be quiet and keep running, woman. I don't need his kind of aggravation."

"You brought him up."

Shay pulled ahead of her and it caused Cassie to pump her legs harder to get back even with her.

She thought about Shay's last comment and wondered why she'd even mentioned the guy. It wasn't as though they'd ever meet again. As they rounded a corner, Cassie focused on the run and didn't let the big hairy man enter her brain.

After they'd separated in the parking lot and tentatively scheduled another run on Friday morning, Cassie drove back to her apartment on Capitol Hill. Her neighbor, Stan, stood in the hallway outside his apartment, with his arms crossed. He wore a bright red silk-looking kimono robe with gold dragons. It seemed too bright for this time of day.

"Hey Stan. Did Jonathan lock you out again?" she asked as she walked toward him.

"No, I've been waiting for you. There's someone in your apartment. I saw him fiddling with the locks and then he just breezed in like he owned the place. Do you have a boyfriend or is he available?"

"What? Why didn't you call the police?" She started to move past him. "How long did he stay in there?"

"Sweetie, he's still in there. I heard the shower come on and banging in the front room. So, you don't have a boyfriend?"

"No and you do. If you hear a gunshot, call the police." She moved down the hall to her door and heard Stan tell her to be careful.

Cassie stopped outside the door and leaned toward it. She could hear music playing and thought she smelled bacon cooking. Her hand moved to her hoodie and she realized she'd left her gun in the holster on the back of her bedroom door.

"Shit," she hissed, put her hand on the doorknob and turned it slowly.

Opening it, she looked past the hallway into the living room and saw a big black leather duffle bag on the floor. It sat open and she saw clothes and a can of Old Spice deodorant. There was a noise from the kitchen and she thought about getting her gun from the bedroom, but didn't really want to shoot anyone in her nice new apartment. She felt it would give the place bad karma.

She lightly stepped toward the breakfast bar that separated the kitchen from the living room. A tall man stood at the stove. His back was bare and he wore a towel around his waist. He flipped bacon and sausages over in a pan on her stove and hummed along with the music playing on her MP3 player. He wiggled his hips in time with the music and started to move his shoulders. His hair was wet and hung down below his shoulders and when she realized it was dark brown, knew exactly who stood at her stove.

"What the fuck are you doing in my kitchen?" she snarled.

Sasquatch turned around. Although he'd shaved off the beard she recognized his light gray eyes.

"Good morning, Miss Holmes. Are you hungry? I'm making breakfast." He smiled and turned back to the stove.

For a second, Cassie was struck speechless. She didn't know what to say and wanted to kick herself for not having a snappy comeback.

"Again I ask, what are you doing in my apartment and why are you wearing one of my towels?" She stepped into the kitchen.

"No, you asked what I am doing in your kitchen. Asked and answered. I can take the towel off if you need it." When he turned, his eyebrow was arched and he grinned. "I should warn you though; I'll have to walk past you to get my clothes. There's fresh coffee in the pot. Why don't you go get cleaned up and we'll have breakfast?"

"You've got more nerve than a bum tooth, Sasquatch. I...you...what...why?" she stuttered.

"Sasquatch?"

"I had to call you something. You never answered my question about your name."

"Ah, right. I'm Jack Donovan." He walked toward her with his hand outstretched.

"Wow, Jack, killer look." She heard Stan say from behind her. "You can take your towel off all you want, Mr. Man."

Cassie looked at her neighbor and wanted to hit him or hit Jack. She couldn't decide which to do first.

"Stan, what are you doing?"

"I had to make sure you were okay and, sweetie, I'd have to say the tall man would definitely have the ability to protect you. If you don't want him, send him down to apartment eleven." Stan fluttered his eyes and swished out of the room.

LAUREN MARIE

"For your information, Stanley, I don't need his protection."

"Keep calling me *Stanley* and you may need protection, babe. I hate that name. Tootles," he said and shut the apartment door behind him.

She looked at the closed door and thought the day couldn't have started any weirder. Something touched her shoulder and she turned to find Jack very close to her.

"Go take a shower and then we'll eat breakfast and talk." He smiled and walked back to the stove.

Chapter Four

Cassie walked into the bedroom, and felt stunned. Who did this guy think he was to just let himself into her apartment, take a shower and turn her kitchen upside down?

She shook her head and pulled her hoodie off. Her gun hung from the back of the door and for a split second she thought about using it to get him out, but couldn't decide how upset she felt that Jack Donovan made himself at home. He'd have a lot of explaining to do.

When the light came on in her bathroom, she saw brown hairs in her sink and the garbage can, and realized he'd shaved his beard off in her space. She cleaned the sink out and decided she really was pissed at this guy.

After she took a quick shower, she dried her hair, put on a pair of jeans and long-sleeved T-shirt and walked out of her bedroom. She saw the towel neatly folded on the breakfast bar counter.

"I hope you like banana-walnut pancakes. It was all I could come up with on such short notice," he said from the kitchen.

She went past him to a cupboard, got a coffee cup and poured. When she turned to him, there were pancakes in the pan and he prepared to flip them over.

"Mr. Donovan, why are you in my apartment?"

He leaned over, opened the stove, took a plate full of bacon and sausages out and set it on the table. "All in good time. Have a seat and I'll explain." Then, he put three of the pancakes onto a plate and went back to the table. "Where do you sit?"

She walked over and sat at a random spot. He'd even set the table, she noticed, looking up at him while he set the plate in front of her. *Apparently, I have a new friend,* she thought sarcastically. He'd gotten dressed and looked good in black jeans and an AC/DC T-shirt.

"I brought syrup or there's some blackberry jam if you don't like generic maple syrup," Jack said as he came out of the kitchen, set his plate down and sat across from her. "I needed a place to get cleaned up and didn't have time to drive up to my house in North Seattle. It would have taken too long. I have court this afternoon. I'll make it up to you."

"Oh great, I can hardly wait," she said.

"Are you always this bitchy in the morning?"

"Only when some weirdo breaks into my apartment, leaves beard hairs in the bathroom sink and takes over the kitchen. Let me guess, you have a record for B and E?" She sat back and stared at him. "How did you get my address?"

"Apologies for the intrusion and, no, I don't have a record. And see, I'm a cop and can usually find people. Eat your breakfast. I promise you'll feel better." He shoved part of a pancake into his mouth and started to chew.

Cassie looked at the plate and had to admit the cakes did look good. "Where'd you learn to cook?" She took a bite of the pancake and her mouth watered.

"It's the single man's curse. I'm not big on fast food and needed to figure out a way to keep from starving to death. I don't admit this to many people, so consider yourself one of the favored few. I've taken cooking classes at North Seattle Community College."

They went silent for few minutes and Cassie picked up a strip of bacon and stared at him. "Have you decided to be more helpful than you were yesterday?" She put the bacon in her mouth and chewed.

"I was helpful. I told you the place you're looking for is dangerous—there are really bad people there—and that you should stay away from it. Sally Skinner is a two-faced liar and if you do go in there, the Powells will be on your back before your next breath. I think it might be a good idea to keep you breathing." He pointed his fork at her and took a sip of coffee.

"Okay, then what would you recommend? I thought about going to the prostitutes strip down by the airport tonight. I've learned there's a section where young girls hang out soliciting and try to pass themselves off as eighteen-year-olds."

She watched him sit back in the chair. His gray eyes didn't break the stare between them and she could see the wheels turn in his head.

"That would probably be a waste of time. If your girl was seen in town on Friday and is being watched by Fred Powell, I doubt he'd let her go that far out of his sight. There's the alley in Sodo that the kids work. You might try that."

"If you know about this alley, then vice must know about it. Why is it allowed to continue?" She set her fork down and put her elbows on the table.

"There's bigger fish to fry out there. Vice follows pros working up and down Highway Ninety-nine, Seatac, Fremont, Licton Springs, even up here on Capitol Hill, but most of the pros up here are gay. The industry has changed so much over the years. It used to be you'd have a pimp who'd have a posse of girls. Now, the gangs have taken over."

"Like the Powells." Cassie sat back in her seat and tried to put together a plan. At the moment all she had were puzzle pieces.

"Like the Powells. Right. They deal mostly in drugs, but that idiot Fred went on-line and bragged about having sweet, young kids to satisfy any taste. It's sick and as much as they are stupid, they do manage to cover their asses."

Cassie found herself second-guessing her plans, which she hadn't done for a very long time. She wanted nothing more than to get Cami Reynolds out of the situation she might be in, but didn't want to get involved with the gangs. Her badge was retired and as much as she'd like to bust the Powells it wasn't her place anymore. She needed to remember she'd hung up her handcuffs.

"Look, I can tell by the crease in your forehead, you're trying figure out your next step. I have to be in court at eleven o'clock and should be finished by one or two this afternoon. How about I pick you up and we'll head down to Sodo together."

"Shouldn't you be working your drug case?"

He laughed. "Guess what? My drug case is the Powells. I've been working it for over six months and according to my next-door neighbor up north, my lawn has taken over the sidewalk in front of my house. I'd really like to finish the case and stay home for a week."

She continued to look at him and wondered why all of a sudden he felt the need to be so helpful. Maybe it was to make up for being an ass yesterday. "What is Sodo?"

He really laughed this time. "How long have you lived here?"

"About three months and, yes, I still feel the need to carry an umbrella."

"That you'll get over the tenth time you run groceries from your car and get soaked. Sodo means south of downtown. It used to mean south of the dome, but since the Kingdome got imploded, it's the first meaning."

"Jack, I have to know. Why, all of the sudden, are you being all helpful and giving me information? Yesterday in the alley, you treated me like some prissy-pink girl. Why are you here in my apartment?"

"Do you want some more pancakes?" he asked, moving back to the stove. He put a couple of spoonfuls of batter into the pan.

"No, I'm fine. Answer my question."

He leaned on the wall between the kitchen and her small dining room. She could tell he tried to form some sort of answer and finally his finger came up with the number one.

"I can tell you're tough. You didn't give in yesterday or back away. I saw you continue to stop people around Safeco Field and even fork over some bucks for information. I just don't think you know this situation well and I'm going to be the superhero and help you. It's nice of me, don't you think?"

"Which superhero? Thor?"

"God, no. I'm Ironman." He grinned and went back to the stove.

"Well, thanks, but no thanks. I have my own way of doing things and don't need Sasquatch around to help." She stood, picked up her plate and went into the kitchen. It hit her that he hadn't made much of a mess. There were splatters on the stove, but that could easily be cleaned up.

"Ah, damn and here I was being so helpful," he said. He put the pancakes onto his plate and went back to the table. "Just admit it, Miss Holmes. You need some help and —viola—here I am." He looked over his shoulder and smiled.

"Okay, if you want to help, pick me up at my office when you're ready. Be forewarned though, if you start being Mr. Bossy, I'll become really honked off and may put you on your ass."

"See, that's the attitude I was talking about. Tough girl. I can work with that." He finished his pancakes and then shooed her from the kitchen.

It impressed her that he cleaned up his own mess. She wasn't sure how to take his offer. She'd had a partner in the past who acted like a he-man and wanted to protect her. She'd worked with him for two years and it just about drove her bats. Her next partner was equal opportunity and much easier to work beside instead of behind. She'd just have to wait and see with Jack.

Chapter Five

Jack finally got released from the court case. He'd testified against a drug dealer, got cross-examined and the DA said he could go. He left the courthouse, found his Jeep Wrangler and started toward Pioneer Square. Once he found the Miss Demeanor's Private Detective Agency building, he drove around the block and looked for parking, which could be a commodity down in this neighborhood. Some of the Pay for the Day lots charged way too much. He found a spot in the alley behind the building.

When he walked through their front door, he almost cracked up laughing. The receptionist wore a bright purple mini-dress, lavender stockings and three-inch clunky shoes with laces. Jack tried to count the number of holes in one of her ears, but then became mesmerized by her black hair with bright blue streaks running through it.

"Good afternoon and welcome to Miss Demeanor Private Detective Agency. How may I help you?" she asked.

"Ah..." He'd forgotten what he was there for. "Oh, right. I'm here to see Cassandra Holmes."

"And you are..."

"Jack Donovan. She's expecting me."

The woman picked up her desk phone and hit a button, smiling up at him. "Cassie, Jack Donovan is here. Very good, I'll bring him back." She hung up the phone and stood. "Follow me, please."

Jack followed the purple girl and walked into a wide open area with four desks. The room seemed really large, but had a nice amount of natural light. He looked to his left and saw, through a glass wall, a conference room with a few windows to the outside. It was where the light came from and he admitted to himself it looked like a nice space.

She motioned to the chair. "I guess since we're going to go to the cathouse together, you'd better start calling me Cassie."

As he sat down, he realized he still wore his tie. He loosened it and took it off, shoving it into his jacket pocket. "About that...We need to make a stop on the way. I have an informant who might have some new facts for you. We'll go from there."

"Who's your snitch?" She stood up and started to put on her jacket.

He saw the holster she wore and the Glock neatly tucked away. It looked like a good weapon and he found himself changing his thinking about this woman. Then he noticed the pleated, mid-thigh denim skirt she wore with black stockings, knee-high black leather boots and realized her holster hung over a red scoop neck T-shirt. For some reason, his mouth went dry. She looked hot.

Earlier, when he'd waited patiently to be called in to testify, he'd thought about Cassie. She seemed smart and tough, but he thought she might have a soft underbelly. He wondered if she really could be tough and make hard decisions. Trying to find a runaway could be frustrating, or so he'd heard. He'd never worked that kind of case, but heard the talk.

Her blonde hair and blue eyes also caught him. Normally, he didn't give women much attention since he was always working, but something in those eyes caught him and he thought he might want to explore it further. He wasn't sure yet.

When she didn't sit back down, he stood. "Someone I trust. He's worked for me the last couple of years."

"Okay. Let's do it." She patted her pocket—for what he had no idea—and came around the desk.

He nodded and followed her toward the front door. When they reached the front office, he heard voices, and saw two women standing by the receptionists desk.

Cassie turned to him. "Jack, these are my partners, Maile Kuhewinui and River Nightingale."

They all shook his hand and he began to wonder about the Miss part of the Agency's name. "You all own this place?" he asked.

"Yes. Our other partner, Shay's going to be annoyed she missed meeting you after Cassie talked about Sasquatch on their run this morning," River said and looked at Cassie.

"He lost the effect by shaving his beard off," she replied.

He felt grateful she didn't mention it was in her bathroom sink that he'd left some of his beard. "We should get going." He put his hand on Cassie's elbow and directed her to the door. "Nice to meet you, ladies," he said over his shoulder and out they went.

Cassie followed him and laughed. "Caught you a little unawares, did they?"

He stopped and turned to her. "Hey, it was all I could do to keep a straight face with your receptionist. How many holes does someone need in their ear?" He turned and continued onto his Jeep.

They moved up the alley where he'd parked and he unlocked the doors with his electronic key.

"Wait a minute. You have a Jeep Wrangler?" Cassie pointed at his vehicle.

"Yeah."

"Huh." She leaned on her hip and shook her head. "So do I, but yours is younger than mine. I have a 2010."

"They handle pretty well when it snows around here. You'll learn how much North westerners freak in the snow if we get any this year."

"I come from Arizona where it rarely, if ever, snows."

They got in, and Jack started it up. It didn't take long to drive past Safeco Field and he felt relieved to find a parking space in front of the bar. They went in and he saw his informant behind the bar. He directed Cassie, to two stools and took a seat.

The bartender walked toward them and when he locked eyes with Jack, the man smiled. "Well, I'll be damned. What rock did you crawl out from under?" The man reached across and shook his hand.

"I've been busy with a case. Mike Donovan, let me introduce Cassie Holmes."

The man looked at her and shook her hand. "If you're dating this hound, I should warn you. He works too much, never calls his mother and sloughs off family gatherings." He continued to shake her hand. "If he bores you, sweetheart, give me a call. I may not know how to cook, but I know the best places for dinner."

"Shut up, Mike. You're gushing." Jack took the man's hand away from Cassie.

She pointed at him and then Mike. "We're not dating. We just met yesterday. Donovan, huh. Are you two related?"

"Mike is my older brother, with emphasis on the *older*." Jack scowled at his sibling.

"Yeah, Jackie's been jealous all of his adult life. The ladies love, love me and can't get enough."

"So this is your snitch?" she asked and kept her voice low.

"Yeah, Mike owns this place and gets all sorts of good gossip, which he passes on to me. Don't you?"

"Only the best in Seattle. What can I get you to drink?"

They both said *coffee* which caused the brother to smirk. After he'd filled the cups, he pointed at a booth and said he'd meet them. They carried their cups over to the dark booth, and he let her go in first and then sat next to her. In a few minutes, Mike joined them.

"So, what can you tell us about Sally Skinner?" Jack said and sipped his coffee.

"What do you want to know?"

"Is she still bringing in kids to ship overseas?" Jack put his arm along the back of the booth behind Cassie.

"No. Ever since the FBI busted that ring a couple of months ago, the trade has dried up. There are groups shipping them from Coos Bay and Newport, Oregon and it's not the big ships. Private boats are taking them, but things up here are a no go."

"Any idea when she runs the kids on the street?"

Mike puffed his cheeks out and let out a breath. "Word has it she brings them down on Friday and Saturday nights to Slut Alley down the road from here, and works them in Beau Peep's. You know the place."

Jack nodded. "Yeah, I know the place."

"What happens to them the rest of the time?" Cassie asked.

"All I know is she keeps them penned up at one of the houses. I did hear that she moved a bunch from Beacon Hill over to a place in Ballard. It's half way between the alley and Highway Ninety-nine. It apparently has a big basement and she keeps them locked up down there with handlers upstairs."

"God, that's sick." Jack shook his head and couldn't believe what he heard.

"Jack, since when are you interested in vice? You can't tell me the drug trade has gone away."

"No, I'm helping Cassie get some information about a case she's working."

"Case? Are you a cop?" Mike looked her.

"Ex-cop. I'm a PI now."

Jack saw his brother's eyebrows shoot up and then he frowned. He knew what was coming and hoped Mike would keep it low.

"Jack..."

"You don't need to go there, Mike. I know what I'm doing."

He saw Cassie look at him, then his brother, and then back at him.

"Cassie, I was involved in a case a few years back that a PI was working. It was a drug case and I never realized the guy fed me crap information. I got busted on the knuckles by Internal Affairs for allowing the guy in on the case. I was suspended for ninety days and got a lot of yard work done at my house."

"They almost ripped you a new one and it wasn't your fault," Mike said.

"Easy, brother. I've forgotten about that and as far as I know Miss Holmes isn't running drugs." He looked at her and saw his hand move to the back of her head and run his fingers through her hair.

She looked at him. "I'm one of those pansy-asses from Arizona," she said flatly.

Jack pulled his hand back and nodded. "Yeah, I said that yesterday, didn't I?"

"You certainly did. However, I can assure you that I don't have anything to do with drugs, then or now. I'm also a pretty honest ex-cop."

Jack sat up straight and pressed his lips together. "That must be why I decided to help you."

Mike slid out of the booth and stood at the end of the table. "It's very nice to meet you Cassie. Jack"—his brother frowned down at him—"keep it in your pants, okay?"

"Asshat."

"Dick-wad." Mike smirked and walked back to the bar.

Jack looked at Cassie out of the corner of his eye and saw her staring at him. "My brother, what a joker," he said sarcastically.

"Joker, right. It did give me an idea." Cassie pushed his shoulder. He took the hint and moved out of the booth.

They walked out into the cool early evening and stopped at his Jeep. After she threw her bag on the hood, she turned her back to him and did something with her skirt. She took her belt off and he saw the back of the thing hike up the backs of her legs. When she turned back around, she'd rolled the waist a couple of times, put the belt over the gathered denim and made herself a really mini skirt. He saw she wore thigh-high stockings, which made his mouth Sahara Desert parched. She then took off her jacket, handed it to him and unclipped her holster. She took her Glock out, put the holster onto the hood and shoved the gun into the back of her skirt. Taking the jacket from his hold, she put the thing around her waist and tied the arms in front of her stomach.

"Now, let's see what we can do to slut *you* up," she said and smiled. "Take your jacket off."

He did as she asked and saw her eyes give him a once-over.

"The button-down has to go. Your black jeans and AC/DC T-shirt will work out better."

His shirt then came off to join her holster on the hood. She handed him the jacket he wore and shook her head.

"No, the business jacket won't do."

"Wait a minute. I may have something else." He unlocked the doors on the Jeep and looked through his stuff on the back seat. His black leather jacket was bunched under his duffle bag and he brought it out. After he put it on, he put his hands out and waited.

"That's really good." She walked up to him and he felt her fingers move under his belt. She pulled his detective badge off and held it up. "This will need to go in the glove box." She backed up a step and tilted her head. "This will do."

"I think I get where you're going, but do you want to fill me in?" He watched her walk back to the front of the Jeep and collect the things off the hood. Running around the vehicle, he opened the door for her.

"We'll walk into Slut Alley and look like we belong there. If we walk in looking like cops, no one will talk to us. You should know that, Mr. Undercover." She set the holster, shirt and her bag on the floor and her hand moved into the bag and pulled out her wallet. She took out about one hundred dollars, turned and put them into his front pocket.

"That's all I have, so if you lose it, I will have to figure out a way to make you pay it back. Do you have any gum?"

He nodded and said, "Glove box."

After she threw his badge into the box, she found a pack of Wrigley's peppermint and took out two sticks.

She chewed it up and got it soft before she started to crack it.

She turned back around. "Ready."

"Do you want to drive over there?"

"How far is it?"

"A couple of blocks."

"No, let's walk. We need to work out our story and learn some signals. Just in case." She smiled up at him. As she started to swish her hips and walk to the sidewalk, she looked over her shoulder. "Don't forget to lock up the car, sugar," she said in a sultry voice.

Jack felt warmth run through his system and thought he needed to know more about the woman.

Chapter Six

As they walked down Occidental Avenue past Century Link Field, Cassie felt excited and nervous all at once. She'd never worked undercover before and would have to act off the seat of her pants. Hopefully, Jack would choose to be helpful. She felt excited because she was actually doing something other than research, on her case, and with luck on their side, she'd get some better leads.

"Have you ever worked undercover?" he asked and put his hand on her lower back turning her down Royal Brougham Avenue.

"No, but I saw something like this in an episode of *Castle* once. I can't do a Russian accent, but I think I can pass myself off as a ditzy blonde." She cracked her gum and smiled up at him. A strange look came over his face. "What?"

"You do remember our conversation this morning?"

"Right, I remember. It's a dangerous place, lots of bad people. Look, if we play our parts right, we can get through the front door and maybe find out some information. Who knows? We may even find Cami." She could tell he felt uncomfortable and put her hand around his waist pulling him close. "We'll just be a couple of perverts looking for a threesome. The younger the better, right?"

She felt his hand move around her waist and saw him look down at her. "I've never done vice before and hate to admit it, but the drug scene is easier. I've been in this place before and there are several cathouses in the building. They're all owned by someone different. The Powells place is at the back."

"You've been there before?"

"Yes and no. Yes, I've been in there as part of a drug transaction and no, I've never sampled the girls."

They turned down First Avenue and continued walking toward a large brick building. It probably was once a warehouse for the docks across the road, but now it looked like a hot nightclub and other people were heading toward it, too.

"Aren't those boots killing your feet?" he asked.

"No, they're very comfortable. Jack, are you having second thoughts?" She worried he'd disrupt her good mood.

"No, we can do this." He looked down at her again, put his hand out and she put hers into it.

When he kissed her palm, she realized he only played his part and then he put her hand on his chest. She admired the fact he wanted to give the impression of a happy, party couple, but it did disappoint her that he hadn't kissed her because of an attraction. She realized where her head was going. She needed to put that on the back burner for now. She groused at herself for being so indecisive. This morning she couldn't stand the guy, but now... *Back burner, back burner,* she thought.

He leaned into her, and nuzzled her neck to play his part, so she grabbed a handful of T-shirt and giggled.

"Oh Jackie, you're such a tease," she said with a sultry-blonde voice and cracked her gum again.

"Baby, you know I just want to show you a good time. This will be a night to remember, my sassy girl." He patted her behind and then his hand parked on her butt cheek.

They walked past a couple of people and continued to snuggle and let their hands wander. Cassie thought they might be overdoing it, but figured what the hell. Her hand moved down over the zipper on his pants and found him hard as a rock.

She snuggled up to his ear. "Is that all for me, baby?"

He'd closed his eyes and laughed. "Yeah, sassy girl. It's all yours," he whispered back.

Jack directed them to a doorway and they walked into the building. She felt amazed at how the place stood out and the vice department did nothing to close it down. From the outside it was just another building, but inside were hallway after hallway of doors with neon lights. They walked toward the back with their arms wrapped around each other and came to the end of a hall. The light above the door read *Beau Peeps,* with a drawing of a little girl wearing a short Little Bo Peep costume. The cartoon character was bent at the waist, looking over her shoulder with her panties showing.

Cassie thought it was sacrilege, but couldn't get pissed about a sign just now. She needed to focus on what opening the door would bring. As they walked through the entrance, Cassie almost cracked up laughing, but it was serious and she needed to stay focused.

Sitting on a stool by a long hallway, was a woman Cassie guessed was Sally Skinner. She looked like a 1950s Lucille Ball wannabe. Her hair dyed candy-apple red and pulled up into a tight bun with tight curled bangs, helped her look the part. She wore a white and red striped dress with chunky white platform shoes. As Cassie and Jack got closer, she could see a thick coat of foundation make-up. The woman must be in her sixties, but obviously tried to look younger.

Sally looked up at them and smiled. "How can I help you folks?"

Cassie cracked her gum and realized Jack wasn't going to say anything. "Hi ya, see, it's my Jackie's birthday and I promised him that he could have anything his heart desired." Cassie looked around suspiciously and whispered, "We heard on the street that you have young, fresh talent and hoped we'd find a little fun. My Jackie's been excited all day about coming here." She kept cracking her gum and saw Sally look him up and down.

"His excitement is apparent." Sally smiled.

Cassie looked at his crotch and gave an annoying cackle. "Yeah, I had to get him warmed up."

"So, are you interested in a threesome?" Sally sat back on her stool.

"Oh no, honey. My baby gets to play by himself, but said I could watch. I want to make sure he's treated right."

The woman stood and adjusted her dress. "Follow me and you can choose your girl."

They walked into a room with about ten girls lounging around. Their clothing was skimpy and a lot of imagination wasn't needed. Sally clapped her hands and the girls moved into a line.

Cassie looked at them all and tried to see if Cami was there, but none resembled the kid.

Sally turned to them. "Have a look and see who strikes your fancy."

As they moved down the line, Cassie got angry. She needed to remember to focus, but it was hard. A couple of the girls were probably sixteen to eighteen, but most of them looked under fourteen.

She continued to murmur comments of "This one's cute" and "She has beautiful hair," to Jack, but when they came to a girl with strawberry-colored hair tied with golden ribbons, Cassie patted Jack's butt and he stopped.

She watched his hand come out and touch the girl's hair. He twisted one of the ribbons around his finger and let it slip away. The poor kid's eyes were as big as saucers as she looked up at Jack who towered over her. Cassie felt guilty and the last thing she wanted was to scare the crap out of any of these kids.

"This one," Jack said and continued to finger the girl's hair.

Cassie let him go and turned to Sally. "What's your charge, honey?"

"Two-fifty for an hour, a buck-fifty for a half hour."

"We'll give you a buck for a half hour. We both know she has very little experience and my Jackie is big. He might have to come in her mouth."

Sally started to laugh, but composed herself. "You're smarter than you look, honey."

"I have to watch out for my babe." She turned to Jack, put her hand in his front pocket and pulled out the one hundred dollars. She handed it to Sally.

"Star, take your clients to room ten. Your time starts when the door clicks shut."

The line-up of girls broke up and the one called Star whispered, "Follow me."

Jack looked at Cassie and crossed his eyes. They followed the kid to a door and went in. The room was the tackiest decor Cassie'd ever seen, with pinks, yellows and sky blue everywhere. She supposed it was meant to feel like a kid's room and give the perverts more of a thrill. Her stomach started to boil and she thought she might be sick.

Jack moved around and she saw him click on a radio, turn it to a rock station and increase the volume.

Cassie looked at the kid and smiled. "Honey, as far as you know, do they record your sessions?"

The girl looked up at her and said, "There's a camera behind the mirror."

She nodded and motioned for Jack to come to her by crooking her finger. He came over and enveloped her in his arms. She nuzzled his neck and said, "Maybe we can put the bedspread over the mirror?"

"You got it." He reached around her and pulled the cover off the bed. After he tucked it around the mirror, he arched his eyebrow. "You're up, baby."

She turned to the one called Star and said in a low voice, "We're not doing anything tonight, so relax, okay?" The girl nodded. "What's your real name?" Cassie sat on the end of the bed and pulled the girl down next to her.

"Amy...Amy Fuller."

"Amy, do you know a girl about your age named Cami?" Cassie asked.

The girl looked at the door and then back at Cassie. "Yeah."

"Do you know where she's being kept?"

"Miss Sally moved her over to Ballard. She's going to walk Highway Ninety-nine."

"I thought she was Fred Powell's favorite?"

"Yeah, she was one of his favorites until she pissed him off. He had her down sucking his cock and she bit him hard. He was furious and Cami got chopped pretty good and sent to Ballard."

"Chopped?"

"Punished."

"You mean beat up?" Jack said.

Amy nodded.

Cassie saw she'd been branded with a tattoo. Part of it showed on her left shoulder and read *FPow*. "What's the tat for?"

"It lets the other people around here know I belong to Mr. Powell." The girl clasped her hands so tight in her lap the knuckles turned white.

"Do you have any idea where the house is located?"

The girl shook her head. "I've never been there, I'm sorry."

"No, don't be sorry. I'll find it." Cassie looked at Jack who leaned against the door. For a split second she thought he looked incredibly hot. She turned her gaze back to Amy. "Sweetheart, does this place have a back door?"

"I don't know. I've never seen one."

"What about guards?"

"There are a couple. They sit in back and watch TV, unless there's trouble. Then Miss Sally calls them out. She doesn't want them hanging around because it's bad for business."

Jack snorted. "It would be bad for something."

"Amy, we're going to leave now. Do you want to come with us?" Cassie saw the kid's eyes well up.

"I'd like to, but I can't. They have my mom and if I don't behave they said she'd be killed."

Cassie looked at Jack. "I got us in here. Do you have any ideas about getting out?"

She could see the wheels turn in his head. He walked closer to them. "Amy, we don't want to get you into any trouble. When we're gone, if Sally asks what happened, tell her I freaked out when you tried to unzip my pants and blabbed something about Sassy being the only one to do that. Improvise if you have to. I know you can do it."

Cassie found a whole new respect for Jack. He really knew where to put his chips. He looked at her and grinned.

"Follow my lead, Sassypants. Ready?" He undid the button on the top of his pants and then took a breath and he bellowed at the top of his lungs, "No! Don't touch me!" He opened the door and pretended to be zipping his pants up and closed the button. "I can't do this, Sassy." He moved down the hallway, stomping his feet.

"Jackie, baby, sure you can do it. I've already paid the money. Why can't you just take her, babe? She's just right for you," she whined.

"It's not you, Sassy. I only want your mouth on my dick. There's nobody like you, baby. I won't do it!"

He continued to shout as they reached the front of the cathouse. Jack caterwauled all the way past Sally Skinner who seemed surprised.

Cassie stood by the woman. "I'm sorry we wasted your girl's time. She really tried. I don't know what's got into my baby."

"The money's non-refundable," Sally said and finally looked at her.

"Fuck, whatever." She turned and followed Jack's bellowing out of the building and onto the street.

They walked at a brisk pace up First Avenue and didn't slow down until they turned on Royal Brougham.

Cassie felt torn. She wanted to go back, and bring Amy out to safety. She wished they hadn't left her, but felt the kid could handle herself. Hopefully, there was a way to bring the Beau Peep establishment down.

She focused so hard on the current situation, that she didn't notice Jack turned them down an alley. Before she could blink, he'd wrapped his arms around her and pressed her against a wall. Her Glock dug into her, but his warm lips against the skin on her neck took all of the attention away from the pain in her back.

When he looked down at her, shock and warmth flooded her body. His hands moved down to her thighs and he pulled her up, moving her legs around his waist.

She put her hands into his hair and grabbed on tight as his lips came down to hers and softly touched and bit her bottom lip.

Their kiss became harder and more passionate as the minutes ticked by. Cassie felt a growing excitement, but her level-headed side put on the brakes. She pulled back, out of breath, and opened her eyes.

"Miss Holmes, you are a brilliant woman," Jack said.

"You're not too shabby yourself, Mr. Donovan. I loved the bellowing." She smiled and kissed him lightly.

"I so want to get naked with you." He nuzzled her neck, again.

"Hmm...I like that idea, but maybe in a couple of weeks when we know each other better and if we actually like one another."

He pulled back and creased his brows. "I like you."

"Jack," she said softly. "Yesterday, I was going to shoot you and this morning you weren't my favorite person on the planet."

"We just started out on the wrong foot. This evening is much better, don't you think?"

"Yeah, I do, but I still have a kid to find and I think we need to cool our jets a little."

He pursed his lips and nodded. "Okay." He let her legs down and stepped back. "I should warn you, I'm not going to make it easy."

Cassie smiled. "I'd expect nothing less."

Chapter Seven

Cassie sat at her desk and tried not to think about Jack. They'd walked back to the agency office and after she'd collected her holster from his Jeep, and turned him down for dinner, he'd given her another hot kiss before they went their separate ways.

At her computer, she checked several different websites and wanted to find the address of the Ballard house. She'd called a computer geek friend down in Phoenix and gave him the information. Now she waited.

She sat back in her chair and stretched, and glanced at her half eaten-bagel. Taking another bite, she picked up her coffee cup and went back to the office kitchen. Just after she'd poured another cup, her phone rang and she hurried back to her desk.

"Tell me something good, Zeke."

"You owe me a salmon. I'm forwarding the house information to your email. Guess whose name I found on the bill of sales?"

"It wasn't under the Powell's?"

"No ma'am. It's under Sally Skinner, only she used another name, Sally Smith. How original, right? It wasn't very hard to trace."

"Great. How'd you figure it out?"

"She used her real social security number on the application. How dumb could she be? The other thing you need to know is she paid cash for the place at that address. Four-hundred and fifty thousand, which makes me think the Powell's are footing the bill. Sally has a checking account in the tank and no savings and her credit history is through the roof."

Cassie saw the email appear. "I got your note. Thanks man, I'll get the fish out to you over the weekend."

"Hey, I only want King or Coho. I don't want any of that Copper River stuff. The last one tasted like broccoli."

"Yes, sir. I won't let you down." She laughed.

After she hung up, she looked at the clock and it was after midnight. She printed the email with the address, shut down her computer and headed for home.

The next morning, Cassie lay on her side and opened her eyes to slits to find out the time. It was six-thirty and she knew she'd have to get up soon. She snuggled down into the warm covers and felt drowsy.

A smile moved across her lips as she remembered the dream that woke her this morning. Jack once again broke into her apartment and for a moment she didn't realize it was him. As she tried to get out of the bed, she couldn't move and was stuck on her back. Then she saw Jack's handsome face as he moved between her legs toward her. When their gaze was even, he'd straddled her hips and leaned over to give her a kiss.

Cassie could remember every touch from that dream and couldn't recall ever having one so vivid. She could still hear him breathing.

Her eyes popped open when she felt something tighten its hold around her waist. She scrambled out from under the hold, moved to her holster on the back of the bedroom door and grabbed the Glock. When she turned to face the bed she caught her foot on something on the floor, slipped back and landed on her butt.

"I don't know who you are, but I'm with the Prescott Sheriff's Department and if you move, I will shoot," she said in an even voice. She got back onto her feet, assumed the stance and heard someone laugh.

Gray eyes looked at her from under the bedding she'd tossed to get up. The comforter came off his head and she saw Jack smile at her.

"Sorry, sweetheart. I didn't mean to scare you so early in the morning," he said. "And, you are in Seattle now, not Prescott."

Cassie dropped the gun down and growled in her chest. "If you don't stop breaking into my..." She stopped and frowned. "Did you straddle and kiss me?"

He propped up on his elbow. "No. I crawled in behind you and, if you didn't notice, I stayed on top of the covers and kept my pants on. However, I might have to strip down due to what you're wearing. I love those panties." He smiled and gave her an eyes-to-thighs look.

Cassie looked down and saw her white tank top and aqua panties. She holstered her gun and grabbed a robe out of her closet. "I swear, I should have you arrested. How long have you been here?"

"I crawled in next to you about three o'clock. You were dead to the world. Man, I knew you'd have great legs, babe. I just knew it," he said and lay back with his hands behind his head.

She stood by the side of the bed and looked down at him with her arms crossed. "What are you doing here?"

"I was all set to head home after I made an arrest in the middle of the night and thought about you and how nice and warm it would be here. I haven't turned the heat on at my house and it's probably very cold."

"I thought you were going back undercover?"

He sat up and looked so hot, Cassie wanted to jump on him. "I told you I stayed on top of the covers. Ha, ha...bad joke. When I got to the precinct last night my captain said I'd been out long enough and wants me to work regular for a while. I went out on a detail and we busted a house lab in West Seattle. I also talked to a friend of mine in vice. Where's your cell phone?"

She nabbed it off her dresser and sat on the bed. He reached by her and picked his up off her nightstand. They both fiddled with their phones.

"Here, put this number in yours." He showed her the screen. "His name is Andy Price and he's expecting your call. His group is going to raid Beau Peep's later this morning."

"What?" She looked at him and grinned. "Really?"

"Yep. He's willing to help you find the Ballard house, too."

She continued to look at him and held up her phone for him to see.

"What's that?" he asked.

"My cell number."

"Oh." He copied the number and gave her the number of his phone. When he finished he leaned on his arm. "Why don't you call Andy and see what he can tell you about the Ballard house?"

Cassie turned her phone over in her hands as Jack rolled onto his side and moved his thighs behind her back. She looked into his gray eyes. "Jack, I already know where the house is located."

His head fell forward and his long hair covered his face. "Is there nothing I can do for you?" he mumbled.

"Hmm...maybe you could make banana pancakes again."

He brought his head up. "You liked them?"

"Yeah and there are still some sausages left-over from yesterday."

"Cass." He moved her hair off her shoulder and let his hand slide down her back. "Don't go to the house alone. I have to go in at eleven o'clock and join another raid on a drug lab this afternoon. I can go with you tomorrow or if you're going to be impatient, I'll call Andy and get you some backup."

"I'm not a cop anymore. I can't just call and say *back me up*."

"Yeah, you can. Andy knows his business and I'm sure he'd be more than willing to help."

"He'll be busy with Beau Peeps."

He hit the button on his cell phone and held it to his ear. "Hey Andy...yep, she's being stubborn. Yeah...do you have someone there, off the clock, who'd back her up?" He went silent for a minute.

Cassie wasn't sure how to take his actions. She stood up and went out to the kitchen to start coffee. She liked that he wanted to help, but she needed to find the kid on her own. It was partly her pride and she thought it would put her thinking straight about making the changes she'd made with her move from Arizona and becoming a business partner. Having watched her associates solve their cases, made her feel a bit on the downside and a win on her first case would give her the kick in the butt she needed.

Jack came into the kitchen and stood in front of the coffeemaker. She finished getting water into the pot and turned off the faucet.

"Andy has a coworker who's willing to help out. Her name's Melanie Mathiason and she'll meet you at the house at eleven o'clock."

"I need coffee," she said.

"She's a good cop according to Andy and knows you're in charge."

"Okay, can I pour water into the maker?" She looked at him and smiled.

"Can I give you a good morning kiss?"

She put the pot on the counter and walked up to him. He put his hand on her shoulder and pulled her into a hug. He looked at her and she felt his fingers touch her lips. Her hands moved to his ribs and when he tilted her head and put his lips onto hers, the tips of her fingers followed the curve of his ribcage around to his back.

Their tongues twirled and she felt his teeth graze her chin and bottom lip. She hugged him and put her forehead on his chest.

"Cassie, promise me you won't go alone." He moved her head up and stared at her eyes. "Promise," he whispered.

"It would seem you've gotten someone to back me up. There's nothing to promise. I won't be alone."

She could see by the look on his face he was concerned, but she wanted to get dressed and head over to the house now. She didn't want to wait until eleven o'clock.

Chapter Eight

Cassie arrived at the house in Ballard just after ten o'clock. She wanted to watch it for a while and parked on a street about a block away. She'd brought binoculars and could see the place clearly. She'd counted four handlers as they moved around the middle floor of the building and it surprised her there were no coverings on the windows. She knew the vice squad and Children's Protective Services were moving on Beau Peeps about now and hoped the men in the house wouldn't get warning calls and try to move the kids.

Her cell phone rang and she lifted it to her ear.

"This is Mel Mathiason. Where are you?"

"I'm parked about a block from the house. The cross-street is 50th. I'm in a beat up Wrangler."

"I'll be there in five."

Cassie saw a red Toyota pull up behind her and in a couple of seconds a tall, dark-haired woman appeared at her passenger-side door. She held up her ID to the window and Cassie waved her into the car. She explained to Mel the way things stood and gave her the plan.

"I really want to get a look at that basement. How would you feel about doing a missionary diversion?"

Mel frowned at her. "I'm not familiar with that one. Is it positional?"

Cassie realized what she referred to. "No, no, not that missionary. I'm talking about religious door bangers. Want to give these guys a come to Jesus moment?"

"It must be a southwestern thing. We don't use it much in vice. Wait a minute, it looks like there's movement." Cassie saw two of the handlers walk out of the front of the house and then the other two. The four piled into a car in the driveway and in a second backed up and went down the street.

"That's too good to be true," Mel said.

"No kidding. Tell you what"—Cassie reached to a duffle bag on the back seat—"here's a walkie. Watch the front and let me know if anyone returns. I'm just going to circle around the place and see if I can tell what's in the basement."

"Andy said I should stick close. You're not a cop anymore."

Cassie looked at the woman and wanted to growl, but knew Mel was right. If she did find anything, it would be best to have a legit cop as a witness. She nodded. "Okay, let's do it then."

They both got out of the Wrangler and started for the house. When they walked side by side, Cassie realized Mel was tall. She looked to be almost as tall as Jack.

When they cut down the drive, Mel went up to the front door and knocked. Cassie continued down the drive, pulled her Glock out and came to a three-foot cyclone fence. This side of the house had no windows to look through. The gate on the fence wasn't locked. She opened it and went quietly into the backyard. The windows in the back were painted over and a door with the top half diamond glass windows was covered, too.

Mel came up alongside of her. "No one is answering the door."

"Stay on the corner and watch the drive. Let me know if those men come back."

"What are you going to do?"

"Don't tell Jack, but I'm going to do a little B and E." Cassie walked up to the door and tried the knob. It was locked. She felt really glad she'd worn a jacket and put her elbow through the diamond closest to the knob. Reaching in, she twisted the doorknob and felt it open. She brought her Glock forward and got a flashlight out of her pocket. After she kicked the door open, she glanced in the opening and saw stairs leading up into the house. There was a doorway under the stairs.

She stood outside the door and listened. There was scuffling on the other side and something clinked. She also heard whispers. Putting her hand on the doorknob, she found it open. Slowly she pushed it and covered the room with her gun. The light from the flashlight showed multiple faces staring back at her.

As she walked through the doorway, she found a light switch on the wall and flipped it on. The light in the room was dim and Cassie guessed they'd probably used forty watt bulbs. About fifteen girls were lined up along the inside wall. Some stood and some sat on the floor on mattresses or mats. They wore T-shirts or tank tops and shorts. There were no shoes and all of them had metal ankle cuffs attached to one of their legs with a chain linking them together. The last girl was attached to a metal ring on the floor.

Cassie lifted her walkie. "Mel, come in here. I need a witness." She moved deeper into the room and felt something hit her forehead. When she looked up, bile came up the back of her throat. There were all types of whips and crops hanging from the pipes in the ceiling. There were so many torture devices and they all moved slightly in the room air.

She went from girl to girl to see how they were health-wise. She heard Mel make a phone call.

"This is badge 1455245. I'm at 5757 White Flat Avenue and 50th. I need backup, CPS and medics.

We've got fifteen victims, all breathing," Mel called it in.

Cassie continued to move down the line. Some started to cry and some were barely conscious. One of the girls lay on her side and watched Cassie move.

She squatted down by the girl. "Hi Cami, how are you holding up?" she asked and saw the golden ribbons plastered into the girl's sweaty hair.

"Not so good. Water, I need water," she croaked.

Cassie looked at Mel who nodded her head and left the room. She touched Cami's head and felt the poor kid burning up. As she lifted the blanket, the kid flinched and Cassie almost broke down crying. The kid's back was bleeding.

"They whipped you?

"Yeah," Cami whispered. "I got chopped for being bad."

"Did Fred Powell do it?"

"Yeah." Cami grabbed at Cassie's hand. "Are you a cop?"

"No, I'm a private detective. Your mom hired me to find you." She could see the girl get more uncomfortable than she already appeared. "Honey, your mom is clean and she left your stepfather." She saw the big brown eyes look up at her. "She's filed for a divorce."

"Ben's gone?"

"Yep, you're going to be safe. I also met Jimmie, Kit and Patrice. They miss you very much." Cassie felt something hit her shoulder and looked at a water bottle. She took it. "Can you sit up?"

The girl moved slowly and Cassie saw more bruises. She opened the bottle and the kid's hands shook so bad she couldn't hold it.

"Here, let me help." Cassie held the bottle up to the girl's lip which was split and watched her take a couple of swallows.

"Do you have any food? I haven't eaten since Friday. Some of the other girls have been longer."

"Help's on the way. We'll get you something soon." Cassie heard sirens and Mel went out to direct the cops after she'd given out all the bottles. "Cami, what do the ribbons mean? I saw another girl wore them in her hair like you."

"It means we belong to Fred and we're his favorites, but I'm not high on his list right now. He's pretty pissed at me."

Cassie followed the ambulance in her Jeep. She stayed with Cami in the emergency room, during the CT scan to make sure the kid had no internal injuries and when a doctor put stitches into some of the deeper cuts on her back. Cami cried and Cassie cried with her. It had been a long time since she'd shed any tears, but Cassie needed to clean out her head.

Cami told her some of the things she'd been made to do, but she'd refused the drugs because she swore with her friends that she'd never do them. Cassie saw the FPow tattoo on the girl's shoulder and felt sick. She hoped the kid would either get it removed or covered by something else.

"You know what?" Cassie asked when they were in a private room. "I think you just became my hero."

"Why?" Cami looked at the IV in her arm.

"You were pretty brave. I admire females who fight for what they believe is right."

"Thanks."

Cassie looked through the open door and saw Emily Cane in the hallway, talking to one of the nurses.

"Cami, I got a taxi to bring your mom here. She's outside. Will you see her?"

The kid looked toward the door. "I guess have to, right?"

"It's totally up to you."

"Yeah," she said and picked at the sheet. "I'll see her."

"Okay." Cassie pulled a card out of her pocket and handed it to the girl. "This is my cell phone number. If you ever need any help or just an ear to listen, give me a call. We'll meet for mochas and just talk. Okay?"

Cami nodded and smiled for the first time. "Thanks."

Cassie watched the mother and daughter reunite and felt good. Her cell phone vibrated in her pocket, something it had done multiple times that day. She knew it most likely was Jack, but she needed to talk to the Child Protective Services representative before she did anything else. She wanted to make sure Cami and her mom got a good counselor.

When she wrapped up the conversation with the CPS rep and felt confident all would go smoothly, she pulled her phone out and hit Jack's number. It started to ring and she could hear it away from her phone. She looked down the hall and saw him walking toward her.

She smiled, when he swooped her up, wrapped his arms around her and held her in a tight hug.

"All Andy knew was you were at the hospital. I think I broke some speed records getting my report written and finding my way over here." He pulled back and looked at her. "Are you all right?"

"Yeah. I'm better than fine. I found Cami, who's with her mother and starting down the road to recovery. There's also some good-looking guy holding me. How could I not be fine?"

"You look exhausted."

She nodded. "I am that."

"Andy said they got Amy out of Beau Peep's and she's in a safe house."

"Did they find out anything about her mom?"

"Honey, you're not going to like it. The mother works for the Powells and sold Amy to them. It's sick."

Cassie leaned against him and couldn't formulate any thoughts. She knew the child-slave trade did this kind of stuff, but it made her heart break. "Have they told Amy?"

"Not as far as I know. CPS will take care of her." He moved his hand over her hair and put his forehead on hers. "I have an offer for you." He arched an eyebrow. "How about you head home and pack an overnight bag? I'll pick you up in an hour."

"I really should head back to the office and write up my report while everything is still fresh."

With his arm over her shoulder, he directed her toward the elevators. "Naw, you can do that on Monday. It's Friday night and I think we should go somewhere with a hot tub and massage and relax. We'll have some good food and I'll explain to you about getting duck webbing between your toes."

Cassie laughed. "You know, that sounds great. What are you up to, Detective Donovan?"

"Never you mind, Miss Holmes. It's a surprise."

As they waited for the elevator, he gave her a kiss. "One hour and we'll be off to nirvana."

Chapter Nine

Monday morning

Cassie walked through the front door of the Miss Demeanor Private Detective Agency. She carried two brown paper bags and smiled at Cory as she walked by the administrative assistant's desk.

"Morning," Cassie said.

"Good morning. You're dripping all over the place."

"Sorry. It's pouring outside." She went into the main office and her three partners looked up from their computers.

"Where the hell have you been?" Maile asked.

"We were supposed to have an agency dinner on Saturday." River stood up and crossed her arms.

"And I waited for over an hour on Sunday morning for our usual run, but you never showed up," Shay said, but didn't look angry. She seemed amused.

"You don't call, you don't write. What gives?" Maile stood next to River and Shay joined the lineup.

Cassie put the bags down on her desk and shed her coat. "It's a funny thing." She walked into the kitchen and grabbed a roll of paper towels and walked back drying off. "After I found Cami on Friday, wrapped things up with CPS, and watched Fred Powell get his nasty old self arrested for underage pornography and child prostitution, Jack sort of whisked me away for a romantic weekend get-away to a very charming little town called Leavenworth. I kept expecting to see a huge penitentiary, but realized I wasn't in Kansas. Anyway this town is really cool and has great gift shops and the Wiener schnitzel was"— she paused and arched her eyebrows—"excellent, but exhausting. Jack taught me the joy of hiking in the rain, getting really cold and then having the best coffee nudges I've ever tasted. He said I'd get used to being wet when my webbing forms between my toes. He showed me and everything. And then I drove him crazy and he contacted his friend in vice and I have an appointment today with CPS to discuss another kid named Amy. It's a long story for another day."

"Wiener schnitzel, huh? Does that mean you and Jack are an item?" River asked.

"Yep, we're trying not to move too fast, but we're exclusive." She pulled a couple of newspapers out of one of the bags. "On another note, have you guys seen the *Seattle Tribune* this morning?" She handed one of the papers to each of them and went back to her desk. "I forgot, you don't read newspapers. Check out the local section, page four."

Cassie wasn't about to tell them she didn't read newspapers either. All of her news was online and if it hadn't been for their neighbor, Stanley, she wouldn't have known about the article.

In the local section was a column entitled: ***Miss Demeanor Private Detective Agency Goes Four for Four.*** The article was about three paragraphs and a very glowing review of their abilities.

"Oh my God, who did they get the information from?" River asked and all four women glanced at each other.

"I thought about that and wondered if maybe our administrative assistant had something to do with it for advertising purposes," Cassie said.

"We'll discuss it in the Monday morning meeting." River continued to look at the article.

"Good and I brought refreshments for the meeting." Cassie picked up the bags and took them into the conference room. When the other three women didn't follow her, she went to the door and leaned on the frame. "I bought fresh, out-of-the-oven scones with orange honey butter from the bakery down the block and the fixings for Southwestern Mimosa's. So get your butts in here, the breakfast bar is open."

"What makes it a Southwestern Mimosa?" Maile asked as she turned into the room.

"It has the usual ingredients with just a sprinkle of my secret sauce." Cassie wiggled her hips and pulled the cork out of the champagne.

"What are we celebrating?" Shay buttered up a scone and took a bite. "Oh, my, this is heaven."

Cassie mixed the drinks in plastic cups. "I thought we should celebrate our first couple of months of business and salute our four successes. One for all and all for one, sort of stuff." She handed each of the ladies a drink.

River held up her cup. "How about we toast *four for four*?"

"I like that, too. Here's to the next four."

They all toasted and sipped and congratulated Cassie on her Mimosa mix.

Shay put her cup on the table and tilted her head. "So, Cass, have you decided you can give up sunny Arizona and deal with the rain up here in Seattle?"

"Yeah. I think I'm in for a long haul and you'll have to thank Jack for that. He really worked hard to convince me over the weekend and thinks our agency is a pretty good group of detectives. Up until now he wasn't a big fan of PI's."

"Did you have to twist his arm very much?" Maile asked and sat down at the conference table.

"I didn't twist his arm at all, but I'll have to say *no comment* to what did get twisted," Cassie said and grinned, but tried to look innocent.

About the Author
Lauren Marie

Lauren Marie lives with her four cats in Western Washington State. She is the author of One Touch at Cob's Bar and Grill - story 3 of the Montana Ranch Series, Love's Touch - Then and Now, Going to Another Place.

Although, she has been focusing her current efforts in the paranormal romance, time-travel and reincarnation genres, she is currently working on continuing the Canon City Series. The first book - Love's Ember's was released fall 2014.

When she isn't pounding the keys, she is an amateur paranormal investigator. She formed her own group in 2006 to hunt ghosts and some unusual experiences have put in an appearance in some of her stories.

Lauren likes to receive feedback. If you want to send her likes and dislikes, you can go to the contact us page on the web-site laurenmariebooks.com or write to her at laurenmariebooks@ gmail.com, themenofhallerlake@hotmail.com. or friend her at facebook.com/laurenmariebooks. She does respond to feedback.

Made in the USA
San Bernardino, CA
11 November 2015